Dear Parent:

Congratulations! Your child is taking the first steps on an exciting journey. The destination? Independent reading!

STEP INTO READING® will help your child get there. The program offers five steps to reading success. Each step includes fun stories and colorful art. There are also Step into Reading Sticker Books, Step into Reading Math Readers, Step into Reading Phonics Readers, Step into Reading Write-In Readers, and Step into Reading Phonics Boxed Sets—a complete literacy program with something to interest every child.

Learning to Read, Step by Step!

Ready to Read   Preschool–Kindergarten
• big type and easy words • rhyme and rhythm • picture clues
For children who know the alphabet and are eager to begin reading.

Reading with Help   Preschool–Grade 1
• basic vocabulary • short sentences • simple stories
For children who recognize familiar words and sound out new words with help.

Reading on Your Own   Grades 1–3
• engaging characters • easy-to-follow plots • popular topics
For children who are ready to read on their own.

Reading Paragraphs   Grades 2–3
• challenging vocabulary • short paragraphs • exciting stories
For newly independent readers who read simple sentences with confidence.

Ready for Chapters   Grades 2–4
• chapters • longer paragraphs • full-color art
For children who want to take the plunge into chapter books but still like colorful pictures.

STEP INTO READING® is designed to give every child a successful reading experience. The grade levels are only guides. Children can progress through the steps at their own speed, developing confidence in their reading, no matter what their grade.

Remember, a lifetime love of reading starts with a single step!

Visit us on the Web!
StepIntoReading.com
www.randomhouse.com/kids
Educators and librarians, for a variety of teaching tools, visit us at www.randomhouse.com/teachers

Library of Congress Cataloging-in-Publication Data
Lagonegro, Melissa.
Outside my window / by Melissa Lagonegro ; illustrated by Jean-Paul Orpiñas, Studio IBOIX, and the Disney Storybook Artists.
p. cm. — (Step into reading)
"Disney/Tangled."
ISBN 978-0-7364-2688-6 (trade) — ISBN 978-0-7364-8085-7 (lib. bdg.)
I. Orpiñas, Jean-Paul. II. Iboix Estudi. III. Disney Storybook Artists. IV. Tangled (Motion picture). V. Title.
PZ8.L1362Ou 2010 398.2—dc22 [E] 2010002134

Printed in the United States of America   10 9 8 7 6 5 4 3 2 1

Disney
Tangled

Outside
My Window

By Melissa Lagonegro

Illustrated by Jean-Paul Orpiñas,
Studio IBOIX,
and the Disney Storybook Artists

Random House 🏠 New York

Rapunzel is a princess
with magic golden hair.

One night,
Mother Gothel takes
baby Rapunzel!
She wants
Rapunzel's magic hair
to make her young.

Rapunzel grows up
in a tower.
Her hair
is very long.

Mother Gothel uses
Rapunzel's hair
to climb the tower.
Rapunzel does not know
that Mother Gothel
kidnapped her.

Rapunzel sees lights
in the sky every year.
She loves to paint them.
She wants to go
to the lights.

But Mother Gothel
says it is not safe.

Flynn is a thief.
Guards want
to catch him.
He must hide.

Flynn finds
Rapunzel's tower.
He can hide there!

Rapunzel finds Flynn
in her tower.
She is scared!

She catches him.

Then she hides him

in the closet.

Rapunzel still wants
to go to the lights.
She asks Flynn
to take her.

Then she will
let him go.
Flynn says yes.

Rapunzel leaves
the tower!

Mother Gothel cannot
find Rapunzel.
She thinks Flynn
kidnapped her.
Mother Gothel is angry.

Rapunzel goes to a pub.

She makes new friends.

She likes

the outside world!

The guards find
Flynn and Rapunzel.
Their new friends
help them escape!

Rapunzel and Flynn
find a cave.
Water fills the cave.
They cannot see!
Rapunzel uses
her magic hair.
It glows and shows
the way out.

Rapunzel sees
the kingdom.

Rapunzel sees a picture.

It shows the King,

the Queen,

and the lost princess.

The Princess has

the same green eyes

as Rapunzel.

Rapunzel sees the lights!
She and Flynn fall
in love.

But Flynn sails away.

Rapunzel is sad.

She goes back
to the tower
with Mother Gothel.

Rapunzel learns that she
is the lost princess!
Mother Gothel
sent Flynn away.

Rapunzel wants to leave.
But Mother Gothel
will not let her go.

Flynn comes
to save Rapunzel!
He cuts her hair.
The magic is gone.
Mother Gothel turns
to dust!

But Flynn is hurt.

Rapunzel cries.

Her tears heal Flynn!

Everyone welcomes
Princess Rapunzel home.
They all live
happily ever after!